PUFFIN BOOKS
POOR LITTLE MARY

Mrs Macintosh is very busy preparing for the class's end of term party. So it is a little while before she realizes that Mary has gone. But soon the entire class is looking for her – in the book cupboard, in the cloakroom, in the playground, in the pond!

The mystery of Mary's disappearance has the school in complete uproar in this wonderfully funny and delightfully observant story.

Kathryn Cave is also the author of *Dragonrise*. She lives in Uxbridge, Middlesex, and is married with three children. Before turning to writing she was a freelance editor.

Also by Kathryn Cave

DRAGONRISE

Kathryn Cave

Poor Little Mary

Illustrated by Kate Aldous

PUFFIN BOOKS

PUFFIN BOOKS

Published by the Penguin Group
Penguin Books Ltd, 27 Wrights Lane, London W8 5TZ, England
Viking Penguin, a division of Penguin Books USA Inc.
375 Hudson Street, New York, New York 10014, USA
Penguin Books Australia Ltd, Ringwood, Victoria, Australia
Penguin Books Canada Ltd, 2801 John Street, Markham, Ontario, Canada L3R 1B4
Penguin Books (NZ) Ltd, 182–190 Wairau Road, Auckland 10, New Zealand

Penguin Books Ltd, Registered Offices: Harmondsworth, Middlesex, England

First published by Viking Kestrel 1989
Published in Puffin Books 1991
10 9 8 7 6 5 4 3 2 1

Printed in England by Clays Ltd, St Ives plc
Filmset in Times (Linotron 202) by Rowland Phototypesetting (London) Ltd

Where oh where is poor
little Mary?
Where oh where is poor
little Mary?
Where oh where is poor
little Mary?
Way down yonder in the
paw-paw patch.

Come on boys, let's go
find her.
Come on boys, let's go
find her.
Come on boys, let's go
find her.
Way down yonder in the
paw-paw patch.

Chapter One

It was the last week of term. Everything was happening.

Children were running in and out of the classroom, arguing, shouting. Mrs Macintosh had a list of things to do before the class party started, a very long list.

There were balloons to blow up.

"Matthew, I've told you before," said Mrs Macintosh. "DON'T pop it."

There was a loud bang. Somebody tugged Mrs Macintosh's elbow.

"What's that, Mary? Good heavens, Matthew, didn't you hear what I said? Well, if you didn't pop it, who did? Sean, is that true?" said Mrs Macintosh crossly. "Was it you who popped Matthew's balloon?"

"No, Miss."

Fiona waved her hand. "It

was Sean, Miss. I saw him."

"Wasn't, wasn't, wasn't."

"All right, that's enough," said Mrs Macintosh. "The next person who pops a balloon goes

home without one. Now, Mary, what did you want?"

But Mary had gone. Mrs Macintosh went back to her list.

There were tables to move to the hall, and glasses to put out. Everybody helped.

"I KNOW you didn't mean to

drop it, Robert," said Mrs
Macintosh. "My goodness,
there's no need to get so upset.
One glass is nothing to cry
about. There: it's all cleared up
already."

There were cakes and biscuits
to take from the kitchen into the
hall.

14

"Simon and Clare, you take the biscuits," said Mrs Macintosh. "Fiona, you take the cup cakes. Well," she said a moment later. "What is it, Fiona?"

"There aren't any cup cakes," said Fiona. "There's only biscuits."

15

"I put the cup cakes out myself not half an hour ago, Fiona," said Mrs Macintosh. "They're on the shelf by the window."

"They aren't, Miss."

They weren't, either.

"All right," said Mrs Macintosh. "Who's taken the cup cakes? Nobody leaves this room until I find them. Matthew, is that chocolate on your fingers?"

"I only had a Penguin, Miss, honest. I don't like cup cakes."

"Sean, let me see your hands.

What's that mark there?"

Before Sean could speak, "I bet he did it," said Fiona.

"You probably took them yourself," Sean shouted. "So there."

"Liar, liar, liar."

"Well, someone took the cup cakes," said Mrs Macintosh. "And all I can say is that if that person ate all twelve of them, I hope he or she is now feeling very sick."

Mrs Macintosh glared at her class and went back to the list.

"Right, I need somebody sensible to help carry in the orange squash." Several hands waved in the air. "No, Clare.

No thank you, Fiona. I know, we'll have Mary. Come on, Mary."

Nobody moved. Mrs Macintosh looked up from the list. "Mary?"

"She's not here, Miss," said Julie.

"She must be." Mrs Macintosh looked round again. "She was a moment ago. I saw her."

"She isn't now, Miss," said Fiona.

Mrs Macintosh looked round

the classroom very carefully.
She thought of all the places
Mary liked.

She looked in the book
corner. There was a book with a
page torn out and one pink
sock.

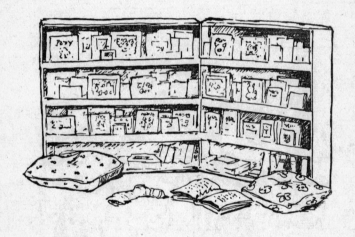

"That's hers, Miss," cried
Fiona. "She always wears them
socks."

Mrs Macintosh put the sock in

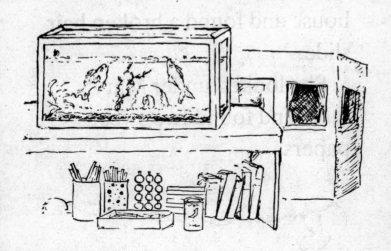

her pocket and went on looking.

She looked by the fish tank. There wasn't anything there but two fat goldfish. There was something floating on the water.

"That's hers, Miss," shouted Lisa. "That's her best ribbon."

Mrs Macintosh fished it out and put it to dry on a chair. She went on looking.

She looked in the Wendy

house and found a broken hair slide.

She looked under Mary's table and found two sweet papers.

There was nowhere left to look but the book cupboard. She had the door half open when Sean tugged her sleeve.

"Mary wouldn't go in there, Miss," Sean whispered. "It's haunted."

"Don't be silly, Sean," said Mrs Macintosh.

Fiona and Clare closed in on her, nodding.

"He's right, Miss," said Fiona.

"There's things in there," said Clare. "Honest. You can hear them. Groaning, like."

"More like moaning," said Fiona.

"Nonsense," said Mrs Macintosh. "It's all imagination."

"I heard it last week in

maths," said Sean.

"I heard it yesterday in reading," said Fiona.

"I can hear it now," cried Clare. "Listen, Miss. Shhssh, everyone. Listen!"

Everyone listened.

"There it is!" Fiona clutched Mrs Macintosh's arm. Mrs Macintosh nearly jumped out of her skin.

"For heaven's sake, Fiona. It's just the wind blowing through the window." Mrs Macintosh shut the cupboard door quickly. "Oh Robert, what's the matter now?"

"I'm frightened, Miss."

Clare and Fiona joined in,

28

sounding gleeful. "I'm frightened too, Miss."

"So am I."

"Is it all green and slimy, do you think, Miss?"

"Do you think it's eaten Mary or just sort of captured her, like?"

Robert started crying, and so did James and Julie.

It took a while for Mrs
Macintosh to get things quiet
again. When she did, someone
else was tugging the sleeve of
her cardigan. "Yes, Lisa?" said
Mrs Macintosh.

"I know where Mary is, Miss.

She's in the cloakroom. I saw
her go."

"For heaven's sake, Lisa, if
you knew, why on earth didn't
you say so?"

"I tried to, Miss, but you
weren't listening. Shall I go and
get her, Miss?"

"All right. Come straight back when you find her, though."

"I want to go to the cloakroom too," said Clare and Fiona.

"Well, go with Lisa, then. But mind you come straight back," said Mrs Macintosh.

Clare, Fiona and Lisa shot out of the classroom.

Mrs Macintosh looked down her list to find what she was supposed to be doing. "Simon, you help with the squash instead," said Mrs Macintosh. "The rest of you sit quietly on the floor until we get back." At the door she turned back looking stern. "And don't forget. I've counted the chocolate biscuits."

Chapter Two

While Mrs Macintosh headed for the kitchen, Lisa, Fiona and Clare were busy elsewhere.

They opened the doors in the cloakroom. They washed their hands with pink soap. They scrunched up paper towels in the sinks.

"Better look somewhere else," said Clare at last. "What about the sick room?"

"What about Mrs Macintosh?" said Fiona. "Someone ought to tell her. You tell her, Lisa."

Lisa didn't want to, but Fiona said someone had to, and Clare said when someone disappeared it was serious.

"It's only Mary," said Lisa, but in the end she went.

When Lisa got back to the classroom, Mrs Macintosh was standing on a table trying to put up streamers. When Lisa waved her hand in the air Mrs Macintosh paid no attention.

"Miss, Mary isn't in the

cloakroom, Miss," Lisa said.
She couldn't reach Mrs
Macintosh's sleeve so she
tugged her skirt instead.

"Wait a minute, Lisa," said
Mrs Macintosh.

Lisa tugged her skirt again,
harder. "Miss, it's important,
Miss. We can't find Mary."

39

Mrs Macintosh was standing
on tiptoe on one foot to tie the
streamer to the rail by the
window. Even like that, she
could hardly reach it. "Later,
Lisa, please," she said.

40

Lisa took hold of the hem of Mrs Macintosh's skirt with both hands.

"Miss," she said. "Mary's DISAPPEARED." She gave Mrs Macintosh's skirt the hardest tug she could, and Mrs Macintosh fell off the table.

"All right, Lisa," said Mrs Macintosh when she got her voice back. She rubbed her knee and her elbow. "I know you didn't mean to. Don't cry, Robert. I'm all right. Nothing's broken. Now, Lisa: what were you saying about Mary?

"But I told you all to come straight back," said Mrs Macintosh, when Lisa had told

her. "Clare and Fiona have no business to go wandering all round the school. Go and fetch them back at once."

"I knew they shouldn't do it, Miss," said Lisa, beaming. "I'll go and get them." Off she went.

"But where on earth is

Mary?" Mrs Macintosh wondered, more to herself than anything.

"Miss, she'll be in the playground, most likely, Miss," said Sean. "That's where she usually goes."

"But she's not allowed in the playground," said Mrs Macintosh. She went to look out of the window. "There's nobody out there. If she was there, I'd see her."

"Not in the bushes," said Sean.

"Or behind the fence round the pond," said Katie.

"Or lying down behind that bank at the side."

"Or crouching behind the roller."

"The best place is the steps outside the cloakroom, Miss, right under the window, where

47

no one can see you."

"Well, well," said Mrs Macintosh sadly. "I didn't know you all got up to things like that."

"Not all of us, Miss," said Sean. "Only Mary."

"But she's so quiet," said Mrs Macintosh. "Most of the time you wouldn't know she was there."

"Yes, Miss," said Sean. After a pause he added: "Most of the time she isn't."

Mrs Macintosh looked at her watch. The party was due to begin in fifteen minutes and she was nowhere near the end of her list.

"James and Sean," she said briskly. "Go and have a quick look outside for Mary. If you see her, tell her to come in at

50

once. If you don't find her, come straight back. No wandering all round the school, understand?"

"Yes, Miss," said James and Sean. Off they went too.

Mrs Macintosh began to count out paper plates and beakers.

Meanwhile Lisa had arrived at the sick room. The only person there was a third year, reading a comic.

"What's the matter with you?" asked Lisa.

"Plague," said the third year without looking up. "Go away

or I'll breathe on you."

Lisa retreated. "Have you seen Mary Fletcher or Clare Robins or Fiona Sanderson?" she asked from the doorway.

"Their bodies are in the pond," said the third year. "So will yours be if you don't get out

of here. Go on. Scram."

Lisa scrammed as far as the cloakroom. There was no point going back to the classroom without Clare and Fiona. Where would they have gone after the sick room?

"The pond!" Lisa exclaimed in triumph. Off she went.

Chapter Three

At the pond Lisa found Clare and Fiona, and Sean and James as well. They were looking at something in the mud at the bottom of the pond. Something black, with a buckle. Something familiar.

"It's her shoe," shouted Lisa. "Mary's!"

56

"Better get it out," said Sean, rolling up one sleeve.

"It's too far in," Clare objected. "You'll never reach it."

"Can you see the rest of her?" asked Lisa.

"No. Could be in among the weeds, though," said James, still hopeful.

Sean knelt on the stones at the side of the pond.

"You'll never reach it," said Clare again.

"Course I will." Sean leant forward and plunged his arm into the murky water.

A minute later a shout went up from near the window in Mrs Macintosh's classroom. "Miss,

Miss, Sean's fallen in the pond, Miss."

Off went Mrs Macintosh like a rocket. Off went all the rest of Class 2 behind her.

By the time everyone arrived, Sean was standing dripping black mud on to the lily pads. In his hand was the shoe. He brandished it at Mrs Macintosh.

"Look, Miss. It's Mary's."

"She must have fell in, Miss,"
said James. "Always mucking
about round here, she was.
She's under them weeds, most
likely."

"Oh no!" said Mrs Macintosh.
"She's not! She couldn't

60

be! It's too shallow. Someone
Mary's size could never . . ."

"I expect the weeds got her,
Miss," said Clare.

"And the leeches," offered
Lisa. "They suck your blood,
leeches do. That pond's full of
them."

"He's probably got them now," said Fiona, pointing at Sean. "Under his shirt and all. Sucking his blood this minute, I bet."

Sean waited hopefully to hear Mrs Macintosh say this was nonsense, but Mrs Macintosh

62

was on her hands and knees peering down into the pond.

"She couldn't be in there," said Mrs Macintosh. "She couldn't."

Sean sat down and began to take off his shirt.

"Oooh, Miss!" cried Clare loud and sudden in Mrs Macintosh's ear. "There's

63

something stuck in the mud
down there. It's a bone, Miss.
Ooh, Miss, it's Mary!"

Mrs Macintosh leant forward
to get a better look and fell into
the pond.

As she came up, draped with

pond weed, "What on earth," said a voice from above, "is going on?"

The Head himself was advancing across the playground with a small, unremarkable girl. She had one

bunch undone and one bare foot.

"Your class party should have started ten minutes ago, Mrs Macintosh," said the Head. "You seem to be running rather late." He was a polite man: he didn't mention the pond weed.

For once Mrs Macintosh ignored him. "Mary," said Mrs Macintosh. "WHERE HAVE YOU BEEN?"

Mary cowered closer to the Head. He patted her shoulder. "I found this poor child," he said, "all alone in the broom cupboard. She was crying, Mrs Macintosh, because she had lost her shoe, her sock and her hair ribbon. Since everyone else was busy, I have been looking after her myself."

"What is that in your hand, Mary?" said Mrs Macintosh.

But it was the Head who answered. "I found a plate of small chocolate cakes, Mrs Macintosh, and little Mary and I shared a couple. I knew you would not mind. They were for the party, were they not?"

"They were," said Mrs Macintosh. She thought but did not say: "All twelve of them." She could clearly see the

chocolate crumbs on the Head's white shirt.

"Well, isn't it time for the party?" asked the Head. "By the way –" a severe note crept into his voice, "someone has stuffed paper towels into the sinks in the cloakroom. I cannot understand how teachers allow this sort of thing. And that boy there –" he pointed at Sean, "is

wearing no clothes. I don't want to know why, Mrs Macintosh. Just sort it out, please, and do it quickly."

The Head gave Mary another pat and headed back to his study. The last two cup cakes were calling him.

"Go back to the classroom, children," said Mrs Macintosh. "All except Mary. No, Sean, the leeches haven't got you. Don't cry, Robert. They won't get you either. Put your clothes on again, Sean, and go back with the others. Thank you, Clare, I can do without any more help from you or Fiona."

"Well, Mary," said Mrs

Macintosh when they were alone. "Have you anything at all to say about what has happened this afternoon?" She bent slowly down to empty out her shoes. "Well, Mary?"

There was a rustle of grass, something that might have been

the patter of small feet, then silence.

"Mary?" said Mrs Macintosh, straightening up. "Where are you, Mary?"

But there was no reply.

Some other Young Puffins

DRAGONRISE
Kathryn Cave

When the dragon Tom found under his bed told him what dragons like to eat best, Tom began to worry. He tried his best to offer his new friend all sorts of tasty morsels as a substitute – but the dragon just didn't seem to be interested. Then Tom's eldest sister, Sarah, did something that Tom could not forgive – and he realized that the dragon could help him take a very unusual revenge!

DODIE
Finola Akister

Dodie the dachshund lives with Miss Smith and Tigercat in a country cottage. He has all sorts of adventures, because he's a very special dog. He is very good at finding things. He finds Miss Smith's key when she gets locked out, he finds Tigercat's new kitten, and he even finds a prickly hedgehog! Life is never dull for Dodie.

HERE COME THE TWINS
Beverly Cleary

Twins are full of surprises: just ask Mr Lemon, the postman. Janet and Jimmy can turn anything into a game, whether it's getting their first grown-up beds, or going to buy new shoes. But what will they do when their next-door neighbour gives them each a dog biscuit? Give them to a dog? No, that would be too easy!

DUSTBIN CHARLIE
Ann Pilling

Charlie had always liked seeing what people threw out in their dustbins. So he's thrilled to find the toy of his dreams among the rubbish in the skip. But during the night, someone else takes it. The culprit in this highly enjoyable story turns out to be the most surprising person.

CLASS THREE AND THE BEANSTALK
Martin Waddell

Two unusual stories which will amaze you. Class Three's project on growing things gets out of hand after they plant a packet of Jackson's Giant Bean seeds. And when Wilbur Small is coming home, the whole street is buzzing – except for Tom Grice and his family, who are new in the street so don't know what the fuss is about, or why people are so nervous!

THE TWIG THING
Jan Mark

As soon as Rosie and Ella saw the house they knew that something was missing. It had lots of windows and stairs, but where was the garden? When they move in, they find a twig thing which they put in water on the window-sill, and gradually things begin to change.

THE WIZARD PARTY

Thelma Lambert

Three stories about the lovable Benny and his mad schemes, which never turn out as planned. For instance, he decides to have his own Hallowe'en party when his friend's party is cancelled, but in spite of careful planning his Dad has to come to the rescue when things start to go wrong.

JAMES AND THE TV STAR

Michael Hardcastle

Two entertaining stories about Katie and James's clever ideas. James has an idea about how to meet his TV hero, and Katie is having a birthday party on the same day as her friend's . . .

BURNT SAUSAGES AND CUSTARD

Marjorie Newman

The twins are sad when Mum says a picnic in the park will have to do for their birthday, but when the day arrives it turns out to be full of surprises and very special indeed!